I0591978

Originally produced 26 December 1994 at

American Stage
St. Petersburg, Florida
John A. Berglund,Executive Director
Victoria Holloway, Artistic Director

Director . . . . .Henry Fonte
Musical Director . . . . .Lee Ahlin
Choreographer . . . . Gary Slavin
Set and Property Designers . . . . .Paul and Sandy Eppling
Costume Designer . . . . Roger Miller
Lighting Designer . . . . Jimmy Humphries
Stage Manager . . . . .Adam Cohen

CAST OF CHARACTERS

Anne Marie Louise De Ville (Cinderella) . . . . .Kimberly Kay
Gaston de Ville, her father . . . . Roger Miller
Arabella de la Terre de Ville, her stepmother . . . . Donnah Welby
Henrietta de la Terre de Ville, her stepsister . . . . .Elizabeth Dimon
Simone de la Terre, her other stepsister . . . . John Huls
Aunt Lula Belle, her great aunt . . . . Hersha Parady
Periwicket, a lizard . . . . Kathy Foley
Nicolas, a mouse . . . . Bonnie Agan
LaFayette, a cat . . . . Ed Lefferson
Hiram Walker Beaufort, The Governor of Louisiana . . Edmund J. Kearney
Clayton Ashley Beaufort, his son . . . . Tom Delling
Beauregard, Clayton's butler . . . . .David Cromwell
The Fairy Godmother . . . . Ricky Wright
First Soldier . . . . .Edmund J. Kearney
Second Soldier . . . . .Jimmy Takacs
Beauregard's Lackey . . . . Dean Muchmore
Ensemble of Soldiers and Ball Guests . . . . . . .Bonnie Agan, Kathy Foley,
Ed Lefferson, Roger Miller,
Christina Moll, Dean Muchmore,
Jimmy Takacs, Alexis Winning

Acting Edition

Cinderella: The True Story

A musical based on CINDERELLA

by Charles Perrault

Book by
Henry Fonte &
Victoria Holloway

Music and Lyrics by
Lee Ahlin

No one shall make any changes in this title(s) for the purpose of production. No part of this book may be reproduced, stored in a retrieval system, scanned, uploaded, or transmitted in any form, by any means, now known or yet to be invented, including mechanical, electronic, digital, photocopying, recording, videotaping, or otherwise, without the prior written permission of the publisher. No one shall share this title(s), or any part of this title(s), through any social media or file hosting websites.

For all inquiries regarding motion picture, television, online/digital and other media rights, please contact Concord Theatricals Corp.

MUSIC AND THIRD-PARTY MATERIALS USE NOTE

Licensees are solely responsible for obtaining formal written permission from copyright owners to use copyrighted music and/or other copyrighted third-party materials (e.g., artworks, logos) in the performance of this play and are strongly cautioned to do so. If no such permission is obtained by the licensee, then the licensee must use only original music and materials that the licensee owns and controls. Licensees are solely responsible and liable for clearances of all third-party copyrighted materials, including without limitation music, and shall indemnify the copyright owners of the play(s) and their licensing agent, Concord Theatricals Corp., against any costs, expenses, losses and liabilities arising from the use of such copyrighted third-party materials by licensees. For music, please contact the appropriate music licensing authority in your territory for the rights to any incidental music.

IMPORTANT BILLING AND CREDIT REQUIREMENTS

If you have obtained performance rights to this title, please refer to your licensing agreement for important billing and credit requirements.

The action takes place in and around New Orleans in 1863.

*All characters, except the Fairy Godmother,
speak in a Southern accent.*

ACT I

Scene One

(We are thirty miles outside of New Orleans. CLAYTON ASHLEY BEAUFORT, the son of the Governor of Louisiana is outside his tent near a battlefield where his Confederate battalion is having difficulty containing the Union Troops. Music and Sounds of battle. BEAUREGARD, his manservant, is helping him change his boots. CLAYTON is very agitated.)

CLAYTON. Beauregard! This is the worse one yet! Criminny! Those Union boys get tougher and tougher!

BEAUREGARD. I don't think The Governor's going to be any too pleased if we don't hold these Yankees here.

CLAYTON. *(Bolting from his stool.)* This is not a good time to mention my father to me!

BEAUREGARD. I know Clayton, give me your other foot.

CLAYTON. I have to get back out there.

BEAUREGARD. You'll do better if you finish changing your boots.

CLAYTON. You're worse than my mother. How on earth will changing my boots help me win this battle.

(He gets up and paces.)

BEAUREGARD. Changing your boots will make your feet think they're not tired. Then YOU will think you're not tired; and you'll go back out there and win the battle.

CLAYTON. THAT is the dumbest thing I've ever heard.

BEAUREGARD. No dumber than going out there with only one boot. Now come here.

CLAYTON. *(He goes back to his stool. BEAUREGARD continues to change his boots. CLAYTON picks up a paddle with a ball attached to it by a string and begins to play with it to relieve his nerves.)* What, in heaven's name, is the second battalion doing? If they don't hold their field we'll all be in big trouble.

BEAUREGARD. *(He is unflappable. Speaks very slowly.)* I know. Give me your other foot.

CLAYTON. Maybe it wasn't such a good idea to attack right now.

BEAUREGARD. It was fine. We'll be back in New Orleans in no time.

CLAYTON. How? The second battalion is doing nothing. We have to push them Yankees across that river. If those second battalion boys don't help a little, we'll never make it to New Orleans!

(He plays with the paddle ball more and more violently, he is very good at it.)

BEAUREGARD. *(Finishes putting on the second boot.)* There, good as new. *(Speaking slowly.)* Give me the paddle ball. *(No answer from CLAYTON. He speaks even more slowly.)* Clayton, give me the paddle ball.

CLAYTON. What?

BEAUREGARD. Give me the paddle ball.

CLAYTON. *(Ignoring him.)* Hey Beauregard, why did the chicken cross the road?

BEAUREGARD. Oh no you don't! This is not the time for one of your stupid jokes! NOW, GIVE ME THE PADDLE BALL!!!

(He yanks it out of CLAYTON's hand.)

CLAYTON. No need to be unpleasant. Maybe I'll give you one for Christmas.

(Enter a SOLDIER.)

FIRST SOLDIER. Clayton! Clayton! Mr. Clayton, sir!

CLAYTON. What is it?

FIRST SOLDIER. It's the second battalion, sir.

CLAYTON. What about it? Did they give up?

FIRST SOLDIER. No sir, they took their field.

BEAUREGARD. They what!?

CLAYTON. Are you sure, soldier?

FIRST SOLDIER. Yes, sir, they pushed the Union troops all the way back across the river.

BEAUREGARD. That's not possible! Just a minute ago they were backed up against them hills.

FIRST SOLDIER. I know sir, but this little girl came out of nowhere and showed them a ravine they could hide in.

BEAUREGARD. Are you drunk, soldier?

FIRST SOLDIER. No sir! *(Music begins.)* The union troops charged; thinking we had given up, and then that little girl led our boys in an ambush.

[HAIL TO THE GIRL]

LIKE AN ANGEL SHE CAME RUNNIN'
KNOWS THIS BAYOU LIKE THE BACK OF HER HAND
WE LAID LOW, THEN THE YANKEES MADE THEIR MOVE
SHE CALLED CHARGE LIKE SHE HAD IT PLANNED

    CLAYTON. *(Spoken)* A GIRL yelled "charge"?
    FIRST SOLDIER. Then she led the command.
    CLAYTON. I don't believe this!
    BEAUREGARD. You saying we won this battle?
    FIRST SOLDIER. Yes Sir!

UNION SOLDIERS FLED TO THE RIVER
GUESS THEY FIGURED WE WERE ON THE RETREAT
TOOK 'EM BY SURPRISE ON THE OLD MISSISSIPPI
WE WERE READY FOR BATTLE; THEY WERE DRAGGIN'
    THEIR FEET
WHEN THEY ALL WENT SWIMMIN', THEN WE KNEW WE
    HAD 'EM BEAT

    BEAUREGARD. What is that infernal caterwauling?
    FIRST SOLDIER. Sir, they're coming this way! They're
bringing the girl to meet you!
    BEAUREGARD. Oh my God! Clayton, you need a clean shirt.

*(He exits. Enter SOLDIERS carrying ANNE MARIE on their
shoulders, singing:)*

    SOLDIERS.
HAIL TO THE GIRL WHO SAVED THE CONFEDERACY
HAIL TO THE ONE WHO LED US INTO VICTORY
NOW THE GRATEFUL BOYS IN GRAY
CAN BE HOME BY CHRISTMAS DAY
ALL HAIL TO THE GIRL WHO SET US FREE

*(ANNE MARIE is put down by the SOLDIERS. She is inspected
roughly by CLAYTON.)*

    CLAYTON. Is this a joke?
    FIRST SOLDIER. On my honor Sir, this is how it happened.

UNION TROOPS NEVER KNEW WHAT HIT 'EM
BY THE TIME THEY LOADED, WE HAD 'EM ON THE RUN

THEY JUMPED INTO THE COLD MISSISSIPPI
THEY WERE TAKIN OFF THEIR BOOTS. THEY WERE
    DROPPING THEIR GUNS
WHEN THEY HIT THE OTHER SIDE, WE HAD THE BATTLE
    WON

ALL.
HAIL TO THE GIRL WHO SAVED THE CONFEDERACY

(SOLDIERS once again raise ANNE MARIE to their shoulders.)

HAIL TO THE ONE WHO LED US INTO VICTORY

ANNE MARIE.
I'M THE BRAVEST GIRL AROUND
NOW WOULD YOU PLEASE, JUST PUT ME DOWN?

ALL.
ALL HAIL TO THE GIRL WHO SET US FREE

*(SOLDIERS begin to parade ANNE around the stage. She continues
    to protest the attention.)*

HAIL TO THE GIRL WHO LED THE BATTLE CRY
HAIL TO THE ONE FOR WHOM WE RAISE OUR BANNER HIGH
THE BATTLE FOUGHT AND WON, NOW A NEW DAY HAS
    BEGUN
ALL HAIL TO THE GIRL WHO SET US FREE

*(At the end of song, bells toll wildly. SOLDIERS cheer, as they put
    her down.)*

SECOND SOLDIER. Speech! Speech!
THIRD SOLDIER. Yes, Speech! Tell us who you are!

(Scattered ad-libs.)

ANNE MARIE. Thank you. Thank you, men. I don't deserve
this. I'm just on my way home from Mississippi. I went there looking
for my father. He and his regiment are missing. They were last seen
near Biloxi. I had no idea I was going to run into this battle. I have to
go. *(Great cries of disapproval from SOLDIERS.)* I have to get back
home.
CLAYTON. *(To SOLDIERS.)* My God! It's true. She is a girl.

(To ANNE MARIE.) If you hadn't driven them across the river we would have lost this battle for sure.

ANNE MARIE. Thank you, sir. But I have to go. I have to get back home.

(Starts to go. He holds her.)

CLAYTON. What do you mean you have to go? We have to take you back to New Orleans to meet my father, The Governor. He'll want to know who you are.

ANNE MARIE. I can't, really. I have to get back home. I was only looking for my father. I've been gone for two months; I have to get home and see if he's come back.

(She takes off. Ad libs from crowd and CLAYTON: "Come back!" etc.)

CLAYTON. Go on, you two, bring her back!

(A great confusion, TWO SOLDIERS attempt to follow her. BEAUREGARD re-enters with a clean shirt. More ad libs from crowd.)

BEAUREGARD. Clayton!
CLAYTON. What?
BEAUREGARD. Here's a clean shirt.
CLAYTON. What for?!
BEAUREGARD. Well, I thought, if they are bringing this girl to meet you, you should look your best.
CLAYTON. She's been here and gone, you ninny! Now, leave me alone!

(Re-enter SOLDIER.)

SOLDIER. She's disappeared, Clayton, sir! She seems to have gone as fast as she came. We couldn't even see which way she went.
BEAUREGARD. All right, so she's lost. Come on Clayton, if we get a move on we can be in New Orleans in time for dinner. I could use a decent meal.
FIRST SOLDIER. *(Begins a triumphant chant.)* Three cheers for this mystery girl! Hip hip hooray! Hip hip hooray! Hip hip hooray! *(Wild cheers.)* Long live the mystery girl!

[HAIL TO THE GIRL - Reprise]

ALL HAIL TO THE GIRL WHO SET US FREE
HAIL TO THE GIRL WHO LED THE BATTLE CRY
HAIL TO THE ONE FOR WHOM WE RAISE OUR BANNER HIGH
THE BATTLE FOUGHT AND WON, NOW A NEW DAY HAS
    BEGUN
ALL HAIL TO THE GIRL WHO SET US FREE

(As the song culminates, the crowd moves off, fading as they go.)

Scene Two

(The courtyard in front of ANNE MARIE's home is revealed. AUNT LULA BELLE, her maiden great aunt, is surreptitiously trying to leave the house. She sneaks out of the door and skulks through the courtyard carrying a bundle of clothes and other prized possessions. It is obvious that she is leaving home. Just as she is about to get offstage, three figures scamper across the stage in the opposite direction. They are PERIWICKET, the lizard, NICOLAS, the mouse, and LaFAYETTE, the cat, ANNE MARIE's pets. They are also packed to leave home. The third figure bumps her. After scaring each other almost to death, AUNT LULA BELLE recovers enough to speak:)

AUNT LULA BELLE. What are you trying to do? Give me a heart attack? What's wrong with you? Where are you going?
ALL THREE ANIMALS. *(Trying to stop her mouth.)* Shhh! Be quiet! She'll hear you!
AUNT LULA BELLE. *(Louder)* What is it?
ALL THREE ANIMALS. SHHHHHHHH!
LaFAYETTE. She'll hear you!
AUNT LULA BELLE. Oh my! I forgot! *(Notices their gear.)* Where are you going?
PERIWICKET. We're running away from home.
AUNT LULA BELLE. *(Very loudly.)* WHAAAAAT!

(All THREE ANIMALS manage to cover her mouth amidst ad libs.)

NICOLAS. Now, if you don't be quiet, we'll have to take you out.

(They uncover her mouth.)

AUNT LULA BELLE. *(Very loudly again.)* But you can't —

(They cover her mouth again; PERIWICKET makes a fist as if to knock her unconscious. She gives a sign that she'll be quiet. Through clenched teeth and sotto voice:) You can't leave home, I'M leaving home.

LaFAYETTE. No, WE'RE leaving home.

AUNT LULA BELLE. Impossible, I've been planning this for weeks. That woman is going to kill me.

NICOLAS. Well she has actually tried to kill ME!

PERIWICKET. And her daughters have tried to kill ME!

AUNT LULA BELLE. But you're her pets! She loves you; you can't leave. Someone has to be here when Anne Marie returns.

LaFAYETTE. Not me!

ALL THREE ANIMALS. We're outta here!

(Music.)

[MISSISSIPPI BOUND]

LaFAYETTE.
WE GOT A SATCHEL, GOT A SUITCASE

NICOLAS.
WE CAN'T TAKE ANOTHER DAY

PERIWICKET.
THAT MEAN OLD LADY AND HER CHILDREN
HAVE FINALLY DRIVEN US AWAY

ALL.
WE GOT NO TIME FOR HANG AROUND
AND SO WE'RE MISSISSIPPI BOUND

LULA BELLE. *(Spoken)* Don't you want to see Anne when she returns? Come on it's not all that bad.

PERIWICKET. *(Spoken)* Ha!

THAT GIRL SIMONE HAS SUCH A MEAN STREAK
LAST WEEK SHE TACKED ME TO THE WALL

LULA BELLE. *(Spoken)* She only wanted to see if you could turn purple.

NICOLAS.
AND HENRIETTA'S GOT A MOUSE TRAP
IN EVERY CLOSET, EVERY HALL

PERIWICKET. *(Spoken)* I don't do purple.

ALL.
THE RUDEST FAMILY YOU WILL FIND
SOUTH OF THE MASON DIXON LINE

YOU GOT THESE WICKED OLD SISTERS THEY'RE RUNNING
    THE PLACE
THEIR MOMMA SCREAMS AND YELLS UNTIL SHE'S BLUE
    IN THE FACE
LIFE WAS SO PEACEFUL BACK WHEN ANNE WAS AROUND
NOW THERE'S ONE THING LEFT TO DO AND THAT'S TO
    HIGH TAIL OUT OF TOWN

WE GOT A SATCHEL, GOT A SUITCASE
WE GOT OUR WALKING SHOES ON TIGHT
NO FORM OF PAYMENT OR PERSUASION
COULD KEEP US HERE FOR ONE MORE NIGHT
THOSE NASTY WOMEN'S GOT US DOWN
AND SO WE'RE MISSISSIPPI BOUND

LULA BELLE. I'll go with you.
PERIWICKET. *(Spoken)* Sorry, sister, you'd only slow us down.

LaFAYETTE.
I WAS NEVER ONE FOR NO LENGTHY GOOD-BYES

NICOLAS.
TIME TO VENTURE OFF TO A NEW ENTERPRISE

PERIWICKET.
SEE YOU LATER ALLIGATOR, AFTER A WHILE CROCODILE

ALL. *(Except LULA BELLE.)*
NOW COME ON, LULA BELLE, LET'S SEE A GREAT BIG
    SMILE

WE GOT A SATCHEL, GOT A SUITCASE
TIME FOR US TO DISAPPEAR
IF WE'RE LUCKY BY TOMORROW

WE'LL BE A THOUSAND MILES FROM HERE
WE NEED A BETTER STOMPING GROUND
AND SO WE'RE MISSISSIPPI BOUND

BYE BYE, SO LONG, WE'LL SEE YOU 'ROUND
RIGHT NOW WE'RE MISSISSIPPI BOUND
MISSISSIPPI BOUND

    AUNT LULA BELLE. Oh, my friends! *(She hugs them.)* I didn't know it was so bad! Go, hurry, before she comes.

(They hug and kiss, then the ANIMALS take their leave amidst many ad-libs. As they exit, AUNT LULA BELLE gathers her belongings once again and begins the slow trek back in the house. Just as she is about to get offstage, ANNE MARIE enters, sees her, and screams:)

    ANNE MARIE. Aunt Lula Belle!
    LULA BELLE. *(Almost having a heart attack.)* Aaaaah! *(Sees who it is.)* Oh! Gracious Heavens, it's you! I'm so glad to see you!

(Much hugging and kissing.)

    ANNE MARIE. Oh, Aunt Lula Belle, I've missed you so much. I'm so glad to be home! *(Realizes that LULA BELLE was on her way somewhere.)* Where are you going?
    LULA BELLE. Not so loud! She'll hear you.
    ANNE MARIE. Who'll hear me? What's the matter?
    LULA BELLE. Will you BE QUIET!!! She'll hear us I tell you.
    ANNE MARIE. This is my house. I'll talk as loud as I –
    LULA BELLE. *(Stopping her mouth.)* Oh no you won't! And this most certainly is NOT your house. Not anymore, it belongs to that witch now.
    ANNE MARIE. What are you talking about? What witch?
    LULA BELLE. If you stop screaming, I'll tell you.
    ANNE MARIE. *(Sotto voice.)* All right.
    LULA BELLE. Well, sugar, I don't quite know how to begin. Your father has taken a new wife in Mississippi.
    ANNE MARIE. What!!!
    LULA BELLE. 'Fraid so. She and her daughters are running the place.
    ANNE MARIE. Daughters? She has daughters? And they're living in my house?
    LULA BELLE. They're living in your room.

ANNE MARIE. What!?

LULA BELLE. They split it right down the middle. Henrietta painted her half green, and Simone painted hers purple. Ask Periwicket about it. He can tell you all about the purple walls.

ANNE MARIE. Purple walls? *(A realization.)* Oh my god, the animals! Where are my pets? I'd almost forgotten about them.

AUNT LULA BELLE. You just missed them, they left.

ANNE MARIE. What do you mean they left?

AUNT LULA BELLE. They just ran away from home. They couldn't take it anymore.

ANNE MARIE. Oh, my poor little friends.

LULA BELLE. That woman is a witch, I tell you; and those girls are two very nasty critters. They broke all your China dolls the first week. And your clothes! Oh, Mercy, your clothes! Everything's in shreds. Imagine the two of them trying to squeeze their fat carcasses into your beautiful dresses.

ANNE MARIE. How can they do that? How can their mother let them? *(Makes up her mind; and starts for the house.)* I'll talk to her, that's all.

LULA BELLE. Be careful! I've met raccoons nicer than them. I sure am glad to see you, my darling. You are as welcome as the flowers in May, but I can't live here any more.

(She starts to go.)

ANNE MARIE. Come back here! This is your home.

LULA BELLE. I'm sorry, dear, you know your father was always my favorite nephew; but I'm going to live with his brother, Travis, in St. Petersburg, Florida. I thought HIS wife was bad, but she's a pussycat compared to this gargoyle. *(Enter ARABELLA, holding a broom.)* Oh, my God! There she is! I'm surprised she's not riding that broom. Don't let her see me!

ARABELLA. Lula Belle, ma cheri, you didn't finish sweeping the dining room, like I asked you. *(Sees ANNE MARIE.)* Who's the tramp you jabberin' with?

LULA BELLE. This, I'll have you know, is my niece, Anne –

ARABELLA. Quiet! You lazy old bag. Now git in the house and finish your work! I'll interview the little ragamuffin myself.

(LULA BELLE scurries back to the house.)

ANNE MARIE. You can't talk to my aunt that way!

ARABELLA. I just did! What do you think you're going to do about it.

ANNE MARIE. You can't talk to ME that way! I am Anne Marie Louise de Ville. My father is Gaston de Ville and you are standing in front of MY house.

ARABELLA. Your house? You don't say? I was tired of hearing about you. I was wondering when you'd turn up.

ANNE MARIE. Turn up? I live here I tell you. This is my father's house.

ARABELLA. Don't make me laugh. Listen to me, you dirty little twit, I am Mrs. de Ville now and this house is mine. You'd better git off my property, or I'll have you whupped.

ANNE MARIE. You'll what? You don't scare me. I have been in the war. I just helped Clayton Ashley Beaufort win a big battle.

ARABELLA. Sure, honey, you're Joan of Arc and Robert E. Lee all rolled into one.

ANNE MARIE. No, but I AM Anne Marie de Ville, and if you think you'll frighten me out of my own house, you have another THINK coming.

ARABELLA. You see this? *(Produces a paper from her reticule.)* This is the deed to this house, signed over to me by your loving daddy. I own this house, lock, stock and barrel; bell, book, and candle. Now, if you want to sign on as scullery maid; we can work something out.

ANNE MARIE. Scullery maid!? My father will never stand for this.

ARABELLA. He ain't here, now is he? Besides I have him wrapped around my little finger. Listen sweets, if you ever want to lay eyes on your daddy again, you'll do as I say. I hope we understand each other. Now, what's it going to be?

ANNE MARIE. You'll never get away with this.

ARABELLA. It seems I already have. And now my little General, I have a little treat for you. Henrietta! Simone! Come on out, girls. I want you to meet our new maid.

ANNE MARIE. Maid? You'll pay me back for this. I swear you will!

ARABELLA. Quiet! Or I'll have you driven out of this house and out of this state. You'll never see your daddy again. *(Enter HENRIETTA and SIMONE.)* Oh, Bonjour mes cheries! *(Back to ANNE MARIE.)* Now let's not have any more unpleasantness, shall we? *(To the GIRLS.)* You both look EXQUEESEETE today. *(Giggles from GIRLS.)* Girls, there's someone I want you to meet. Someone who MIGHT be working for us for a while. If she behaves herself.

ANNE MARIE. But I tell you that this is my –

ARABELLA. Quiet! Henrietta, Simone, this is your new maid. And by the way, she says she's your long, lost step-sister. *(GIRLS react to ANNE MARIE's distressed state.)* I know she's a little dirty,

and a far cry from her father's description, but girls, where are your manners? Henrietta?
HENRIETTA. *(Grudgingly)* Enchante.
ARABELLA. Simone?
SIMONE. Charmed, I'm sure.

(The GIRLS cannot control themselves and get a case of the giggles.)

ARABELLA. Girls, girls where is your charité?
SIMONE. *(Suddenly serious.)* I'm not moving out of that room.
ARABELLA. Oh dear me, no. I'm sure we can set up a nice cot for her in the kitchen. That's where she'll be spending most of her time. Or maybe she can bunk in with that old Lula Belle if she wants.
ANNE MARIE. Now, just a mo –
ARABELLA. Remember, if you ever want to see your daddy again, you'll do as I say. *(ANNE MARIE is cowed.)* Now, here's a list of your chores for today. *(Hands ANNE MARIE a very long list.)* Girls, stay right here, I'm going inside to freshen up and put on my new hat. Remember we have an appointment, in town, for those new dresses. Don't spoil your nails. I'll be right back.

(She exits.)

HENRIETTA & SIMONE. *(Very sweetly.)* Oui, oui, mamá.

(As soon as ARABELLA is out of sight they both stick their tongues out in her direction and have another simultaneous attack of the giggles.)

ANNE MARIE. *(Interrupting their merriment.)* Well, girls, this is not going to be easy for any of us, but let's make the best of this situation. *(She extends her hand to HENRIETTA.)* My name is Anne Marie Louise.
HENRIETTA. *(Extends her hand, then withdraws it at the last minute.)* Who cares?

(More laughter.)

ANNE MARIE. Simone, I've lived here all my life, and if we're going to be sisters, I think we should –
SIMONE. Can it, sweetheart!

(They both stare at ANNE MARIE, whom they begin to circle viciously. ANNE MARIE is silent.)

HENRIETTA. So this is daddy's little darling, is she?

SIMONE. *(To HENRIETTA.)* The most beautiful girl in New Orleans, remember?

HENRIETTA. She is beautiful. She's the belle of the ball. Look at her elegant clothes.

SIMONE. The latest styles from Paris, I'm sure.

HENRIETTA. What are those charming britches called?

SIMONE. Oh Henrietta, look at her stunning complexion. She must work all day to get that beautiful gray tone.

HENRIETTA. What is this gorgeous shade of rouge called? Cinder flush?

SIMONE. A sight to behold!

HENRIETTA. Oh Daddy was right, she IS a sight!

SIMONE. Daddy's not only old and stupid, he's blind!

(Peals of laughter.)

HENRIETTA. I must touch that beautiful skin. *(She approaches, and is about to pinch ANNE MARIE's smudged cheek, when ANNE MARIE bites her finger.)* Yeeaowww!

(HENRIETTA does a little dance of pain. SIMONE attempts to come to the rescue and charges ANNE MARIE.)

SIMONE. You bit my sister ...

(ANNE MARIE expertly deflects her and twists her arm behind her back.)

ANNE MARIE. You shouldn't have said that about my father. *(She shoves SIMONE into HENRIETTA who is just recovering from her bite. They both go down.)* I've been in the war, you nitwits! What do you think? That I like looking like this? That I roll around in the mud and cinders for the fun of it? I just helped win the battle for New Orleans!

SIMONE. Yeah, sure tell us another whopper. You just like being dirty. You're just a pig.

(ANNE MARIE goes for her again. Both GIRLS scramble.)

HENRIETTA. Careful Simon, the little piglet has a mean bite.

ANNE MARIE. I tell you, I've been in the war! Otherwise I would be dressed and cleaned up as nice as you . Nicer actually.

SIMONE. Sure, Miss Jefferson Davis here is not only a war hero, but she's the belle of the ball.

HENRIETTA. Yeah, the belle of the cinder ball. Cinder Bella!
SIMONE. No, you mean Cinderella. That's much more romantic.
HENRIETTA. Cinderella, the war hero.
SIMONE. Cinderella, the beauty queen!

(Both GIRLS begin to circle ANNE MARIE, being very careful to stay out of her reach. They taunt her, and begin chanting at her: Cinderella, Lady of Smudge, Cinderella, Queen of Dirt, Cinderella, Princess of Mud, etc.)

ANNE MARIE. Stop it! That's not my name! Stop it! I'll make you sorry you ever laid eyes on me or my house!

(The circling and taunting degenerates into real fistcuffs when ANNE MARIE catches SIMONE and brings her down. Just as HENRIETTA is about to jump on the two of them, BEAUREGARD enters, exhausted.)

BEAUREGARD. *(Sees the melee.)* Girls! Girls! Break it up! Break it up, I tell you! There's enough fighting all around us. Now stop! *(He manages to break them up, but not before suffering a few blows in the process.)* Come on, I'm not in the mood for this, I didn't get any dinner. Now, as you know, there has been a great battle just outside the city in which our troops, under Clayton Ashley Beaufort, have prevailed.
HENRIETTA & SIMONE. *(Swooning at the mention of CLAYTON's name.)* Clayton! Oh Clayton!
BEAUREGARD. Quiet! New Orleans is safe, for now. The Governor, The Honorable Hiram Walker Beaufort III, is throwing a magnificent Ball tomorrow night at the Hotel Ponchartrain in honor of his son Clayton; and also in honor of the mystery girl who helped him win the battle. *(Both girls eye ANNE MARIE suspiciously.)* I come to deliver an invitation – *(SIMONE and HENRIETTA lose all control and squeal with delight.)* Will you be quiet!!! An invitation to all the unmarried young girls in and around New Orleans. I'm not sure you three wildcats qualify. But it's not up to me, is it? The real reason for the ball is to try to discover the identity of this mystery girl who helped Clayton win the –
ANNE MARIE. *(Very simply.)* I am that girl.
BEAUREGARD. If I had a dollar for every –
HENRIETTA. She's a liar! I am the girl! I just got back from the front.
SIMONE. No! She's a liar! I'm the girl who won that battle.
BEAUREGARD. I know. I know. You are all the girl. It is amazing how many war heroines there are suddenly in New Orleans.

The battle was only this morning and so far there has been at least one brilliant Confederate General in every house and plantation I've been to.

ANNE MARIE. But I'm telling you the truth, you could ask me questions about –

BEAUREGARD. I know, honey, save it for the Governor.

ANNE MARIE. But I –

BEAUREGARD. *(Stopping her.)* And I do not need to tell you that Clayton is the most eligible bachelor in this state. And that he is very interested in this girl.

(Peels of laughter from SIMONE and HENRIETTA who go wild. BEAUREGARD begins to exit as ARABELLA is entering in reaction to all the noise.)

ARABELLA. What is all this noise? What have you done to my girl you huss ... *(Sees BEAUREGARD.)* huss ... huss ... hospitable young thing?

BEAUREGARD. *(To ANNE MARIE.)* Who is THIS dragon?

SIMONE. This is our mamma, the lady of the house.

HENRIETTA. *(With great emphasis.)* Arabella de Ville. MRS. Gaston de Ville.

ARABELLA. *(Eyelashes aflutter.)* Charmed, I'm sure.

BEAUREGARD. *(To ARABELLA.)* Save it! *(To ALL.)* Like I said: Tomorrow night, eight PM, The Hotel Ponchartrain. Be there. *(To ANNE MARIE.)* Try to look like something, will you?

(He's off. As soon as BEAUREGARD is off, SIMONE and HENRIETTA go crazy telling ARABELLA about the invitation. They are hysterical and making no sense.)

ARABELLA. Wait a minute! One at a time.

HENRIETTA. We've been invited to the Governor's Fancy Ball tomorrow night.

SIMONE. At the Hotel Ponchartrain. We'll be introduced to Clayton Ashley Beaufort! Oh, Clayton!

BOTH GIRLS. *(Highest pitch.)* Ahhhhhh!

ARABELLA. Quiet Girls! We have work to do. Landing such a husband is serious business; take it from me. Not a minute to waste. In the house everybody.

HENRIETTA. *(Starting for the house.)* Can you believe it Mama. It's a dream come true: The Governor's Ball!

SIMONE. *(Following)* With nice young men; not dirt farms like back home in Mississippi. Mamma, you were so right. *(It sinks in.)* We've been invited!

ANNE MARIE. *(Before ARABELLA can respond.)* We've ALL been invited. Every young unmarried girl in New Orleans has been invited.

(A petrifying silence as they realize that ANNE MARIE means to go. All three do a very slow take to ANNE MARIE.)

ARABELLA. Excuse moi?
ANNA MARIE. The man said all unmarried young girls were invited. I am an unmarried young girl. I am invited. Besides, the ball seems to be in my honor. The least I can do is go.
SIMONE. *(To ARABELLA.)* She tried to tell the man that she was the mystery girl that every one is talking about.
HENRIETTA. That's after she bit me and pushed Simone.
ARABELLA. Did she?
SIMONE. Cinderella's not a very nice girl, Mama.
ARABELLA. Cinderella? That's a wonderful name for a maid.
SIMONE. *(Very proud.)* I gave it to her.
ANNE MARIE. That's not my na –
ARABELLA. Quiet! My little girl is right. Cinderella is not a very nice girl – and girls who aren't nice don't go to balls, do they?
ANNE MARIE. That's not fair! The man said ALL girls. You can't keep me from going.
ARABELLA. We'll see about that. What would you wear? You have no clothes. How would you go; unless we took you in our carriage.
ANNE MARIE. YOUR carriage?
ARABELLA. Besides, you have too much to do.
ANNE MARIE. I tell you, it's not fair!
ARABELLA. And I tell you what, toots. You git all your chores done and you do everything my gorgeous little girls need to look even more exquisite for the ball; and we'll see about letting you go. Maybe that lame brained aunt of yours can rustle up something for you to wear. There's an old set of curtains around here somewhere. *(To SIMONE and HENRIETTA.)* Let's go girls, we have serious work ahead of us. *(To ANNE MARIE.)* We all do. *(As they exit.)* I knew those tiaras would come in handy ...

(They run into the house. ANNE MARIE is left alone for a moment. She's about to burst into tears; instead she stomps her foot and defiantly says:)

ANNE MARIE. I'll show you. I can do anything I set my mind to. As God as my witness, I'll get to that ball one way or another!

(Music begins. She runs into the house. Just as she enters, SIMONE comes to the upstairs window.)

[WHERE IS CINDERELLA]

SIMONE. Where is Cinderella?
HENRIETTA. I thought she was with you.
SIMONE. Someone has to curl my hair.
HENRIETTA. Someone has to help me choose a dress.
SIMONE. Where is she? She was just here ...
HENRIETTA. I don't know where she went.
   ARABELLA. And don't forget, dear, we have to have the copper polished, and dust the chandelier and after that ... CINDERELLA! CINDERELLA! Well, where has she gone?

   HENRIETTA.
I NEED TO CHOOSE FROM ALL THESE DRESSES
WHICH ONE WILL CATCH THE GUV'NOR'S SON
I'LL HAVE TO DO SOMETHING WITH THESE TRESSES
WHERE IS CINDERELLA? CINDERELLA, I NEED YOU.
   WHERE IS CINDERELLA?

   SIMONE.
PERHAPS I'LL WEAR A NEW CREATION
SOMETHING GRAND WITH JEWELS AND LACE
A GOWN BEFITTING OF MY STATION
CINDERELLA! CINDERELLA! WHERE IS CINDERELLA?

   HENRIETTA.
I NEED TO HAVE MY CORSET LAUNDERED
I NEED TO CHOOSE FROM ALL THESE SHOES
I NEED THAT GIRL WHERE HAS SHE WONDERED
WHERE IS CINDERELLA? CINDERELLA COME QUICKLY!
   WHERE IS CINDERELLA?

   SIMONE.
MY POOR FEET ARE GETTING BLISTERS
SEARCHING UP AND DOWN THESE HALLS
WHERE'S THAT DWEEB, I MEAN WHERE'S MY SISTER?
CINDERELLA! CINDERELLA! WHERE IS CINDERELLA?

   ARABELLA.
THE EFFORT MUST BE DO OR DIE
TO MAKE THESE GIRLS PRESENTABLE

MAYBE THEY'LL CATCH THAT CLAYTON'S EYE
CINDERELLA! CINDERELLA! WHERE IS CINDERELLA?

SIMONE. *(Spoken)* Have you seen her?
HENRIETTA. *(Spoken)* No, it's getting late.

(ARABELLA and the girls sing the last lines of their verses together. In the musical bridge, ANNE MARIE is revealed in the kitchen, hard at work.)

ANNE MARIE.
WELCOME HOME, NOW SCRUB THE FLOORS AND WASH
  THE DIRTY CLOTHES
AND DON'T FORGET THE GLOP BEHIND THE STOVE
WHEN EVENING COMES, THEY'LL GO TO FANCY PARTIES
  AND BALLETS
I'LL SIT AT HOME AND DREAM MY TIME WILL COME
  ANOTHER DAY
ANOTHER DAY
ANOTHER DAY

ARABELLA. *(Spoken)* Cinderella, I need you immediately!

(SIMONE and HENRIETTA repeat their verses back to back simultaneously, while ANNE MARIE sings ANOTHER DAY, and ARABELLA sings the following:)

ARABELLA.
WE'VE JUST RECEIVED AN INVITATION
TO THE GOVERNOR'S FANCY BALL
THIS WILL CALL FOR PREPARATION
CINDERELLA? CINDERELLA? WHERE IS CINDERELLA?
THE EFFORT MUST BE DO OR DIE
TO MAKE THESE GIRLS PRESENTABLE
MAYBE THEY'LL CATCH THAT CLAYTON'S EYE
CINDERELLA? CINDERELLA? WHERE IS CINDERELLA?

Scene Three

(The kitchen. 6:30 P.M. the next evening. ANNE MARIE is alone. She is working very hard at cleaning out the fireplace.)

[WELCOME HOME]

ANNE MARIE.
WELCOME HOME
AND THANK YOU FOR YOUR BRAVERY IN THE WAR
NOW KINDLY WASH THE LAUNDRY, SCRUB THE FLOOR
WELCOME IN
YOU MAY HAVE NOTICED THINGS ARE SLIGHTLY
    CHANGED
YOUR FATHER'S GONE AND LEFT YOU WITH THREE
    STRANGERS
THANKS A LOT

GALLANTLY
I WAS FIGHTING FOR LIBERTY
RIGHTEOUS CAUSES THEN
SUDDENLY
THE HEROINE WHO LED THE GRAND CRUSADE
BECOMES THE COOK, THE SEAMSTRESS, AND THE MAID
ALL AT ONCE
I'VE TRADED IN A BANNER FOR A BROOM
WITH ORDERS TO DEFEAT THE DIRT IN EVERY ROOM

ALL ALONG
HOME'S THE DREAM THAT WOULD KEEP ME STRONG
HOME'S THE PLACE WHERE I ONCE BELONGED
BUT NO MORE
WITHOUT A HOME, TELL ME WHAT'S THE FIGHTING FOR.

(Enter LULA BELLE with a mountain of clothes.)

LULA BELLE. All right, this is the last of the laundry. *(Sees ANNE MARIE, who is exhausted.)* Now, honey, take it easy. You'll kill yourself.

ANNE MARIE. I just have a little more to do. Scrub these pots, sweep out the fireplace, mop the floor, polish the silver, beat the rug, shoe the old mare, and trim the front hedge, then I can go.

LULA BELLE. But, honey, you'll be too tired. It's already six-thirty. Besides, what will you wear?

ANNE MARIE. I can't think about that now. I'll think about that later. Put that stuff on the table and help me shovel these cinders out of this fireplace.

LULA BELLE. I can't believe it. You cleaning out the fireplace. This is terrible. You've already cleaned the whole house, and helped those two bimbos get dressed. What more do they want?

ANNE MARIE. Don't worry about that now. Just give me a hand, PLEASE, I don't have much more time.

LULA BELLE. I can't move. I'm too tired. YOU'RE too tired. You're going to make yourself sick. We've been at this all day! What good will it do?

ANNE MARIE. *(Going to her.)* Come on Aunt Lula Belle! You can sleep the rest of the night. I just have to get to that ball! *(LULA BELLE gets up and they begin to shovel cinders from the fireplace together. While the women have their heads in the fireplace, LaFAYETTE, NICOLAS, and PERIWICKET enter, one at a time, not seeing then and making sure that the coast is clear. LaFAYETTE motions the other two in front of the fireplace. Just when they get there, the women finish their work and turn out from the fireplace.)* Now there. *(They bump into the three animals. A wild melee ensues. Much noise. Fur flies. Finally they all recognize each other.)* Oh, it's you three. I have been so worried about you. *(Hugging, kissing, ad-libs.)* Aunt Lula Belle told me you had left home.

LaFAYETTE. *(Looks at PERI.)* We didn't get very far.

PERIWICKET. Don't blame me. You got us lost.

LaFAYETTE. Well how could I concentrate with Nicolas whining about being hungry the whole time?

NICHOLAS. It's not my fault. It hasn't been safe to eat anything around here lately. There are mouse traps everywhere!

ANNE MARIE. It's all right boys. We're just happy to see you.

NICHOLAS. Maybe we should hide. I'm still scared.

LULA BELLE. We're all right for a while. Those three harpies are glued to their mirrors: trying to make themselves beautiful. And I tell you, it's a dirty job.

LaFAYETTE. Oh, Anne Marie, It has been so awful without you. There's something really wrong with them.

NICHOLAS. They are trying to kill me!

PERIWICKET. *(To LULA BELLE.)* Did you tell her about the wall incident?

LULA BELLE. No, I started to but –

ANNE MARIE. I know, boys, it hasn't been a day at the beach for me either.

LaFAYETTE. Now that you're here, everything will be all right.

PERIWICKET. Yeah, kick them out, Anne Marie!

NICHOLAS. We've certainly had enough!

ANNE MARIE. Boys, for the moment, I'm afraid that I can't do anything. They've kind of kicked me out. I'm the scullery maid until further notice.

ALL THE ANIMALS. What?!

(Ad-libs)

SIMONE. *(O.S.)* Cinderella! *(The ANIMALS scamper.)* I need my curls combed out.

ANNE MARIE. False alarm, boys. I'll be right back.

(She goes.)

LaFAYETTE. Cinderella? Who's that?

LULA BELLE. Oh that's the new name those two creeps have given her, because she was covered in ashes and dirt when she got here.

PERIWICKET. But that's not her name.

NICHOLAS. That's terrible. We have to do something!

LULA BELLE. Oh, boys, I'm so worried about her. She hasn't stopped since yesterday. They don't believe she's the girl who won the battle ...

ALL THREE ANIMALS. *(Ad-libs, all at once.)* What battle? It's her! The battle for New Orleans! Oh, I knew it!

LULA BELLE. Yes it's her. That's where she's been. Now Arabella has told her she has to finish everything on this list before she can go to the ball tonight. We'll never get it done. They're leaving in the carriage at seven. It's almost seven o'clock now and there's still so much to do. We've got to figure out a way for her to get to that ball. If she can talk to the Governor, everything will be all right.

LaFAYETTE. *(Taking charge.)* OK boys, here we go; we have a lot of work to do: Nicholas, you finish cleaning the ashes from the fireplace, Peri, you and Miss Lula Belle start folding those sheets, I'll start on the silverware; we can do it!

(A wild flurry of activity as they all go to work.)

ANNE MARIE. *(Entering)* Well, those girls look as good as they're going to look ... *(Sees them at work.)* Oh, boys, thank you so much. Did Aunt Lula Belle tell you? *(Nods and ad-libs of assent.)* This means so much to me. We don't have much time, but we can do it!

(She plunges in, helping NICHOLAS with the fireplace.)

ARABELLA. *(O.S.)* Cinderella! *(At the sound of her voice the ANIMALS scamper, the laundry flies, and there is a wild chase while they find places to hide. They overturn furniture, throw clothes, and in general make the room look worse than it was. ARABELLA enters, dressed for the ball.)* Cinderelly, hon. *(Sees her at the fireplace.)* Ah, your face in the ashes again, naturallement. Are you ready for the ball?

ANNE MARIE. Almost.

ARABELLA. *(Surveying the situation.)* It doesn't look like it to me. This place is a mess. YOU are a mess.

ANNE MARIE. I can be ready in no time. I can clean the kitchen tomorrow morning.

ARABELLA. Oh no, you don't. I think you'd better forget this whole thing. It's seven o'clock. You didn't keep your end of the bargain. The work isn't done. YOU are not done. The carriage is waiting; and we are leaving right now.

ANNE MARIE. Oh, please don't leave without me, step-mother; I just have to see The Governor about father's regiment. I'll do anything you want.

ARABELLA. A bargain is a bargain. I kept my half and you have let me down. I'm sorry, but what kind of an example would that be for my little girls if I let you get away with a stunt like this.

ANNE MARIE. Oh please, step mother, please take me with you!

ARABELLA. Sorry. Please make sure that all this work is done when we get back or you'll find yourself out on the street tonight.

LULA BELLE. Now you listen to me ...

ARABELLA. Quiet! Now I mean it. All the work gets done or I'll throw you both out! *(Sweetly)* How does my new hairdo look? *(She starts out.)* Come on girls! In the carriage! We don't want to keep Clayton waiting. Now let's see, which one of you is going to be Mrs. Clayton Ashley Beaufort? *(Back to ANNE MARIE.)* Au reservoir!

(She's offstage. Squeals of delight from the girls [O.S.] as they leave the house. Finally the front door slams. There is an awful moment of silence. Then ANNE MARIE falls on the floor sobbing. AUNT LULA BELLE and the animals try to comfort her to no avail. She is inconsolable. This goes on for a few seconds, then ...)
(There is a loud crash and puff of smoke. They are all thunderstruck. The FAIRY GODMOTHER appears. She looks very puzzled. She is a Jamaican woman in full fantasy Jamaican costume. She speaks in a heavy Jamaican accent.)

ANNE MARIE. Who are you?

FAIRY GODMOTHER. This is most peculiar, I was flying from my home in Jamaica to the big party in Barbados, when my direction finder went haywire and pointed straight to New Orleans.

ANNE MARIE. Who are you? What do you want?

FAIRY GODMOTHER. *(Stepping down to them.)* Well child, if I could tell – *(The animals go berserk as she approaches them. A wild hysterical scene ensues.)* Oh settle down! *(They are very quiet; she surveys them.)* Interesting menagerie. Where AM I?

ANNE MARIE. About four miles outside of New Orleans. This is the home of Gaston de Ville. I am ...

FAIRY GODMOTHER. *(Cutting through.)* O.K., who's in trouble here?

ALL. *(Ad-libs)* What? What are you talking about? etc.

FAIRY GODMOTHER. There's someone in big trouble here; or I wouldn't have been diverted.

ANNE MARIE. I don't really know ...

FAIRY GODMOTHER. All right, I haven't got all day. Speak up! The Voodoo King gets mighty upset if I'm late to his shindig. Or is that the Mambo King? I always get the two of them mixed up.

PERIWICKET. But who are you?

FAIRY GODMOTHER. I'm a Fairy Godmother; what does it look like I am?! You know, where I come from, lizards are a lot smarter.

PERIWICKET. Well, there's no need to be ...

FAIRY GODMOTHER. So, WHAT IS IT? I'm here to help.

LULA BELLE. Tell her, honey.

ANNE MARIE. Well, I don't quite know how to begin ... You see, my daddy ...

FAIRY GODMOTHER. Look, darling, I don't need your life's story. What's this whole song and dance about your Papá. What's the problem NOW?

ANNE MARIE. Well ...

LaFAYETTE. *(Interrupting)* You see Fairy Godmother, it's like this: Anne Marie here has just come back from the war.

(Ad-libs, etc. telling the story:)

LaFAYETTE.	**NICOLAS.**	**PERIWICKET.**
and no one believes that she won the battle of New Orleans, which of course, she did. Anne Marie can do anything she set her mind to do; except maybe get to this Ball tonight.	And her daddy re-married in Mississippi to this really horrible woman with two horrible daughters; and they have horribly come here to live. And they are trying to kill me!	And her ugly ugly step-mother will not allow her to go to the Governor's Ball tonight!

FAIRY GODMOTHER. Quiet! *(The ANIMALS are subdued.)* This is all about getting to a little party?

(The ANIMALS begin again:)

LaFAYETTE.	**NICOLAS.**	**PERIWICKET.**
Well, this is not just any party ... etc.	Anne Marie is not necessarily a party girl ... etc.	You haven't been paying attention here, have you ...

FAIRY GODMOTHER. Don't even start! *(ANIMALS are quiet again; to ANNE MARIE.)* Look, sweetheart, this ball is really important to you, isn't it?

ANNE MARIE. Yes, but ...

FAIRY GODMOTHER. How do you think I got here?

ANNE MARIE. Well, it seems that your direction finder is on the fritz ...

FAIRY GODMOTHER. No. Don't be a wiseacre. You brought me here. You had stopped listening to your heart. You had stopped believing in yourself. You had given up. That is a challenge no self-respecting Fairy Godmother can pass up. Not even subconsciously. Now, we must get you to that ball!

ANNE MARIE. But how can I ever go to the ball? Look at me!

FAIRY GODMOTHER. You're right; it will be a challenge. *(Resolves to do it.)* Well, I didn't bring my kit with me so we'll have to improvise. *(Music begins.)* Ya know?

ANNE MARIE. Improvise?

FAIRY GODMOTHER. We'll have to make it up as we go along. Use whatever we can find.

[A LITTLE O' DIS, A LITTLE O' DAT]

FAIRY GODMOTHER.
A LITTLE O' DIS, A LITTLE O' DAT
WE GONNA MAKE YOU THE BELLE O' DE BALL IN NO TIME
    FLAT
A WAVE O' DE WAND, A MAGICAL SPELL
YOU'LL BE SITTIN' IN A CARRIAGE WAVIN' FARE-DEE-
    WELL

YOU GONNA NEED SOME TRANSPORTATION
TO HELP YOU GET AWAY
THAT PUMPKIN OVER THERE WILL FILL DA BILL

PERIWICKET. Did she say "pumpkin"?
LaFAYETTE. Yes, I believe she did ...

FAIRY GODMOTHER.
IF WE CONCENTRATE COMPLETELY
AND SAY THE MAGIC WORD
THEN TURN AROUND AND CLOSE YOUR EYES
INSTANT SEDAN DE VILLE

Calabazas locomotus.

(The pumpkin explodes. Lights and sound change. A beautiful carriage is revealed.)

LaFAYETTE. Let's have a look.
PERIWICKET. The act is impressive.

FAIRY GODMOTHER.
A LITTLE O' DIS, A LITTLE O' DAT
WE GONNA MAKE YOU THE BELLE O' DE BALL IN NO TIME
　　FLAT
A WAVE O' DE WAND, A MAGICAL SPELL
YOU'LL BE SITTING IN A CARRIAGE WAVIN' FARE-DEE-
　　WELL

YOU'RE GONNA NEED YOU SOME HORSE POWER, A STEED
　　MIGHTY AND STRONG

NOW'S THE TIME WE HAVE TO IMPROVISE
WE TAKE YOUR LITTLE FRIENDS HERE
AND WAVE THE MAGIC WAND
AND WE CHANGE A CAT AND MOUSE TO HORSES
RIGHT BEFORE YOUR EYES

Ratus. Felinus. Equitatus. *(NICOLAS and LaFAYETTE are transformed into magnificent horses.)* Oh, I love my work! Now let's see, that's a pumpkin to a carriage, a mouse and kitty to horses. I guess that covers it. I want you to have the time of your life tonight my little ...

ANNE MARIE. Fairy Godmother, I'm very grateful for all you've done, but I can't go to the ball like this.

FAIRY GODMOTHER. Of course, what a silly goose! I'm gonna take care of that for you right now.

NOW WHAT WAS MOTHER THINKING
WE NEED SOMEONE TO HOLD THE REINS
YOU THERE! WE GONNA TEACH YOU HOW TO DRIVE

PERIWICKET. Me? How?

FAIRY GODMOTHER.
JUST SAY "YA!" WHEN YOU GET GOING
AND SAY "WHOA!" WHEN YOU WANNA STOP
KEEP YOUR SEAT BELT FASTENED
DON'T GO OVER FIFTY-FIVE

PERIWICKET. But Fairy Godmother, I'm a lizard.

FAIRY GODMOTHER. Oh yeah, we'll see what we can do about that.

PERIWICKET. I'm happy being a lizard ... no wait!

FAIRY GODMOTHER. Reptilius Conductoris! *(PERI is transformed into the driver.)* Your carriage, mademoiselle. Climb aboard.

ANNE MARIE. Fairy Godmother, have you ever been to a ball?

FAIRY GODMOTHER. You kiddin' sweetie? Where do you think I'm going now!?

ANNE MARIE. What's wrong with this picture?

FAIRY GODMOTHER. Oh! My Goodness! You'll have to change your clothes.

ANNE MARIE. That's what I'm trying to tell you. I don't have any other clothes!

FAIRY GODMOTHER. Well, why didn't you say so in the first place?

WE'RE GONNA NEED AN UGLY SHMATA

Something old and gross. What you got on will do just fine.

ANNE MARIE. Thanks a lot.

FAIRY GODMOTHER.
NOW STAND RIGHT HERE BESIDE ME
AND RAISE YOUR HANDS UP HIGH
THEN TURN AROUND AND ROUND AND ROUND
YOU'RE GONNA BE DRESSED TO THE NINES.

Vestitus Transformatus!

(ANNE turns around three times to the fairy music and her tattered rags are transformed into an exquisite ball gown right in front of the audience.)

ANNE MARIE. Oh, it's beautiful! Thank you Fairy Godmother. *(FAIRY GODMOTHER hands her a pair of glass slippers.)* And glass slippers, too!

FAIRY GODMOTHER. All in a day's work, honey, but there's one downer, so listen up. I go off the clock at midnight. Understand?

ANNE MARIE. Not really.

FAIRY GODMOTHER. Look, my magical powers are good for a day at a time. When the clock strikes twelve, everything goes back to how it was. Your chauffeur is a lizard, your carriage is a pumpkin, your horses are dog meat, and you go back to the rag look, so you MUST be home by midnight.

ANNE MARIE. I will. I promise.

FAIRY GODMOTHER. Good, honey, have yourself a great time!

EVERYONE.
A LITTLE O' DIS, A LITTLE O' DAT
AND WE MADE YOU DE BELLE OF DA BALL IN NO TIME
    FLAT
A WAVE O' DE WAND, A MAGICAL SPELL
AND YOU'RE SITTIN' IN A CARRIAGE WAVIN' FARE-DEE-
    WELL
AND YOU'RE SITTIN' IN A CARRIAGE WAVIN' FARE-DEE-
    WELL
AND YOU'RE SITTIN' IN A CARRIAGE WAVIN' FARE-DEE-
    WELL

FAIRY GODMOTHER. Don't forget! Home by midnight!

ANNE MARIE. *(As the carriage moves off.)* Thank you! I won't forget!

END OF ACT I

ACT II

Scene Four

(A hall or a room in The Hotel Pontchartrain. CLAYTON enters playing with the paddle and ball again. He is wearing loud boxer shorts and a tank-top tee shirt. He is singing a silly song as he plays. He is very good at the paddle game.)

CLAYTON.
PREEP PAH PEEP PAH PEEP PAH, POOM,
DOO DAH, DOO DAH,
PREEP PAH PEEP PAH PREEP PAH POOM,
DOO DAH DEE DOO DEE DAY.

DOO DAH DEE DOO DEE DAY
DOO DAH DEE DOO DEE DAY
PREPP PAH PEEP PAH PREEP PAH POOM
DOO DAH DEE DOO DEE DAAAAAAAAAY.

(Repeat as necessary, then: Big Finish Enter BEAUREGARD, unseen by CLAYTON, from the opposite side, checking a list. Sees CLAYTON's state of undress. Becomes very agitated.)

BEAUREGARD. Clayton!
CLAYTON. *(Startled)* Whaaaat!
BEAUREGARD. What are you doing?
CLAYTON. Are you trying to kill me? You scared me to death! What does it look like I'm doing?
BEAUREGARD. Do you know what time it is?
CLAYTON. Half past the monkey's ...
BEAUREGARD. *(Stopping him.)* Clayton! It is almost eight o'clock! In about three minutes, your father is receiving everybody who is anybody in New Orleans in that Ballroom. It's the big Fancy Ball; and YOU are in your underwear!
CLAYTON. I'm not going.
BEAUREGARD. What do you mean, you're not going?
CLAYTON. Just what I said, I'm not going.
BEAUREGARD. Oh yes you are.

(He heads off into the wings.)

CLAYTON. *(In the general direction.)* Oh no I'm not. And don't you come back here with my clothes. Everyone thinks I won that battle. No one really believes me about the girl. Why is that? I hate dressing up, anyway. I hate fancy balls. I hate New Orleans. I hate this hotel. I want to go back to Baton Rouge.

BEAUREGARD. *(Entering from the opposite direction with CLAYTON's suit on a rolling valet.)* You know very well we are not going back to Baton Rouge until after the Ball. And certainly not until we find out who this mystery girl is. Did you take a bath today?

CLAYTON. I swam in the lake. Take it or leave it.

BEAUREGARD. I'll take it.

(BEAUREGARD starts to put CLAYTON's shirt on him.)

CLAYTON. Hey, Beauregard, what's the one thing you can't eat for breakfast?

BEAUREGARD. Oh no, you don't.

CLAYTON. Come on, come on!

BEAUREGARD. *(Resigned)* All right, what is the one thing you can't eat for breakfast?

(BEAUREGARD begins to ready the shirt so that CLAYTON walks right into it.)

CLAYTON. Lunch! *(No response from BEAUREGARD.)* Get it? Breakfast? Lunch? *(Still nothing from BEAUREGARD.)* Boy! Nobody laughs at my jokes. *(CLAYTON turns around to say this to BEAUREGARD and walks right into the outstretched shirt.)* That's another reason I'm not going to the stupid ball. Everybody is a phoney. And, besides, that girl isn't going to show up. *(He realizes BEAUREGARD has put the shirt on him.)* I'm not going.

BEAUREGARD. *(Trying a different approach.)* Alright, alright, tell me a joke.

(BEAUREGARD begins to set up the pants so that CLAYTON will walk into them.)

CLAYTON. You mean it?

BEAUREGARD. Yes, come here though.

CLAYTON. *(As CLAYTON gets into telling the joke, BEAUREGARD begins to put his pants on.)* O.K., O.K. What do you get when you cross a bathing suit with two elephants? Ready?

BEAUREGARD. Yes.

CLAYTON. Swimming trunks! Get it?

BEAUREGARD. I take it back. Don't tell me any jokes.

(BEAUREGARD has managed to put CLAYTON's pants on him. Music begins.)

[I GOT A MILLION OF 'EM]

CLAYTON. *(Is off and running.)*
WHAT DO YOU GET WHEN YOU CROSS A CAT WITH A LEMON?

BEAUREGARD. I'm sure I don't know.

CLAYTON.
WHAT DO YOU GET WHEN THOSE TWO THINGS COMBINE?
WHAT DO YOU GET WHEN YOU CROSS A CAT WITH A LEMON?

BEAUREGARD. What?
CLAYTON. A sour puss.
BEAUREGARD. That was very nice. Now let's finish dressing. Oh look, it's your fancy coat. Your favorite!
CLAYTON. Oh, good. I love a good coat joke. *(He grabs the coat and dances off with it.)*

WHAT DO YOU GET WHEN YOU CROSS A MINK WITH A KANGAROO?

BEAUREGARD. I couldn't begin to tell you.

CLAYTON.
WHAT DO YOU GET WHEN YOU PUT THOSE TWO TOGETHER?

BEAUREGARD. Go ahead, tell me.

CLAYTON.
WHAT DO YOU GET WHEN YOU CROSS A MINK WITH A KANGAROO?

You get a fur coat with very large pockets.

BEAUREGARD. Clever.

CLAYTON.
I GOT A MILLION OF 'EM
HOW I LOVE TO TELL A JOKE
I GOT A MILLION OF 'EM
AND I LOVE THE FUN I POKE
EVERY DAY I'M FACED WITH POMP AND ARISTOCRACY
LIFE'S TOO SHORT TO TAKE SO SERIOUSLY

(CLAYTON has, without realizing it, put on his coat.)

BEAUREGARD. Now look in this mirror, Clayton. You might want to do something about that hair.

CLAYTON. *(Musses up his hair horribly.)* How about this?

BEAUREGARD. Come on, we really don't have time for your silly jokes.

CLAYTON. The world would be a better place if we did have time for some silly jokes. Everybody is too concerned with how we look and not with what each person has inside. *(Grabs the mirror.)* I wish there was a mirror that reflected a person's heart, brains, talent, wit or goodness. That, my dear Beauregard, would be something. *(Tosses the mirror to BEAUREGARD who has to dive to catch it.)* Hey, I got one; listen to this.

WHAT DID THE ONE EYE SAY TO THE OTHER
WHEN ONE EYE SPIED THE OTHER, WHAT DO YOU THINK
    TRANSPIRED?

BEAUREGARD. *(Clenched teeth.)* We really don't have time for this, Clayton.

CLAYTON.
WHAT DID THE ONE EYE SAY TO THE OTHER?

BEAUREGARD. Tell me.

CLAYTON. There's something between us and I think it smells.

BEAUREGARD. Don't you ever get tired?

CLAYTON. No! *(CLAYTON does a complete strip-tease during the next chorus and takes off everything that BEAUREGARD has managed to put on him. He is back to boxer shorts and tank top.)*

I GOT A MILLION OF 'EM
HOW I LOVE TO TELL A JOKE
I GOT A MILLION OF 'EM
AND I LOVE THE FUN I POKE

EVERY DAY I'M FACED WITH POMP AND ARISTOCRACY
LIFE'S TOO SHORT TO TAKE SO SERIOUSLY

BEAUREGARD.
WHAT DO YOU GET WHEN THE GOV'NOR'S SON IS LATE
   TO THE FANCY BALL?

CLAYTON. That's the spirit. What?

BEAUREGARD.
WHAT DO WE GET IF I HAVEN'T DONE MY JOB?

CLAYTON. I don't know. Tell me, tell me.

BEAUREGARD.
WHAT DO YOU GET WHEN THE GOV'NOR'S SON IS LATE
   TO THE FANCY BALL?

CLAYTON. I give up.
BEAUREGARD. Beauregard is out of a job and Clayton is doing K.P. for a week.
CLAYTON. That's not funny.
BEAUREGARD. You're darn tootin' it's not funny. And that is exactly what is going to happen if you don't get these clothes on and get in that ballroom. Now, why won't you cooperate?
CLAYTON. Because I don't want to GOOOOOO!
BEAUREGARD. Why don't you want to go to the Ball? It's the biggest event of the year.
CLAYTON. No, it's not. It's the same as every other party I have to go to. You think it's easy being the governor's son? All these stupid people talking to me; when I know they really think I'm a geek. None of them care about me. They are just trying to get to my father.
BEAUREGARD. Well, do something different. Be unique. Demonstrate your talent for telling jokes. Act however you like. *(Falls to his knees.)* Just please put your clothes on and go!
CLAYTON. Maybe that's what I'll do. I'll tell jokes. Everyone should have to demonstrate a talent. We'll have a talent show.
BEAUREGARD. Fine. Put on your pants.
CLAYTON. That'll shake them up. Hey, what did the dancing banana do at the talent show?
BEAUREGARD. The split?
CLAYTON. How'd you know?
BEAUREGARD. Lucky guess.

CLAYTON.
I GOT A MILLION OF 'EM
HOW I LOVE TO TELL A JOKE
I GOT A MILLION OF 'EM
AND I LOVE THE FUN I POKE
EVERY DAY I'M FACED WITH POMP AND ARISTOCRACY
LIFE'S TOO SHORT TO TAKE SO SERIOUSLY
I SAID LIFE'S TOO SHORT TO TAKE SO SERIOUSLY

CLAYTON & BEAUREGARD.
OH YEAH

CLAYTON. One more. One more. Why couldn't the skeleton go the Fancy Ball?
BEAUREGARD. I give up.

(He starts offstage.)

CLAYTON. *(Yells after him.)* Because he didn't have any BODY to go with.
BEAUREGARD. AHHHHHHH!!!

(He is off.)

CLAYTON. Get it? Skeleton? Body? Boy! I wish, just once, that SOMEONE would laugh at one of my jokes! *(CLAYTON is still center stage in his boxers and tank top when the drop behind him flies off revealing a tableau vivant of a magnificent Ball already in progress. There are various couples frozen in mid-dance. A waltz. He realizes where he is.)* Oh my God! *(Covers himself.)* Beauregard! Help!

(He runs offstage.)

Scene Five

(As CLAYTON clears the stage, the ball comes to life. The couples dance a short waltz: WALTZO DEL CORNEO. At the end of it, everyone applauds and moves off center stage. BEAUREGARD enters up center and:)

BEAUREGARD. Ladies and gentlemen! The Governor of Louisiana, The Honorable Hiram Walker Beaufort.
GOVERNOR BEAUFORT. *(Enters and takes a bow. The crowd applauds.)* Thank you, thank you ladies and gentlemen. Let's

hear it for the orchestra! Mr. Lee Ahlin and the Rebels! *(alt: Xavier Cougar and the Bayou Panthers.)* Yes sir! What a thrill it is to have y'all here tonight. It gives us great pleasure to see y'all enjoy yourselves so much at our annual Fancy Ball. *(More applause.)* This year, of course, we have even more to celebrate. New Orleans is still safe from the Yankee invaders! Yes sir! *(Cheering and applause.)* And we seem to owe it all to a little mystery lady. Yes sir! A little girl whom I hope will come forward tonight. Maybe she is one of you! *(Ad libs from crowd.)* And now, it gives me great pleasure to introduce to you, my son, fresh from battle, Clayton Ashley Beaufort. *(Everyone turns up center to the entrance where nothing happens.)* My son, Clayton. *(Nothing. Sotto voce to BEAUREGARD:)* Go see where the distracted little angel is, will you? *(Back to the crowd.)* I'm sure he'll be right here. Have another drink. Maybe we'll have another dance.

(Just as the orchestra is about to begin BEAUREGARD appears up center.)

BEAUREGARD. Ladies and Gentlemen, Mr. Clayton Ashley Beaufort!

(He reaches in and yanks a somewhat dishevelled CLAYTON out into the BALL. He turns and starts to bolt.)

GOVERNOR BEAUFORT. CLAYTON!
CLAYTON. *(He decides he'd better stay.)* Yes, Daddy. Good evening everybody. How nice to see you.

(He heads towards his father. Just as he is getting to him, BEAUREGARD enters up center and announces:)

BEAUREGARD. Ladies and Gentlemen, one of our newest citizens, a recent arrival from Mississippi, Mrs. Arabella De Ville. *(Enter ARABELLA, who attempts to flirt with BEAUREGARD on her way in. He withers her with a look. There is much murmuring from the crowd. She makes a bee line for the GOVERNOR.)* Ladies and Gentlemen, Mrs. De Ville's daughters; by a previous marriage, I might add, Miss Simone de la Terre. *(Enter SIMONE, looking like she would, to continued murmuring from the crowd.)* And Miss Henrietta de la Terre.

(Enter HENRIETTA, dressed even more extravagantly than her sister. The murmuring of the crowd peaks here. Music begins and the crowd dances again.)

ARABELLA. Here I am, mes cheris! Come here. *(The girls have a long giggly cross to where the GOVERNOR and CLAYTON are trying in vain to disentangle themselves from ARABELLA's firm grip.)* This, girls, is Governor Beaufort. *(Giggles)* And this, is Mr. Clayton Ashley Beaufort. *(More giggles.)* Gentlemen, these are my daughters Simone and Henrietta. Tres jolly, n'est ce pas? Well Governor how about a drink for a nice lady? A lovely mint julep perhaps? What do you say?

GOVERNOR BEAUFORT. Yes, my wife will be ...

ARABELLA. Governor, how you talk! I just meant we should let these young people get acquainted.

(She yanks the GOVERNOR off.)

CLAYTON. *(A desperate attempt.)* Daddy, I'd like a drink too! *(The GOVERNOR just growls at him as he is led off. He surveys his prospects.)* Well, here we are.

HENRIETTA. Nice Ball.

SIMONE. Yes.

CLAYTON. Yes.

HENRIETTA. *(Looking at the dancers.)* Nice dance.

SIMONE. Oh, yes. Very nice.

CLAYTON. Yes, Our butler Beauregard is in charge of all dances. Dancers run in Beauregard's family. Too bad they don't dance! *(He howls. The girls don't get it and are deadpan.)* Get it? Run? Dance? It was a joke?

SIMONE. Oh, ha ha ha.

HENRIETTA. Very funny.

CLAYTON. Wait. I have another one. My cat can talk.

SIMONE. Really.

HENRIETTA. How nice.

CLAYTON. Yes, yesterday I asked what two minus two was; and she said nothing. *(He laughs; no response from girls.)* Get it? Nothing? Two minus two? She said: "nothing"? *(Only puzzled looks.)* Oh, boy.

(There is a fanfare. BEAUREGARD enters up center.)

BEAUREGARD. Ladies and Gentlemen, your attention please! We have a mystery guest! *(Reaction from crowd.)* No great ball would be complete without one. We have a young lady who refuses to identify herself. Since all young ladies are invited to this year's Governor's Fancy Ball, here she is: Our Mystery Guest!

(Fanfare. Loud murmuring from the crowd. Enter ANNE MARIE. The crowd is stunned into silence by her beauty. CLAYTON is

dumbstruck. He drops SIMONE and HENRIETTA and slowly walks up center to her. He stands silently before her for a few seconds just drinking in her beauty. The two sisters run and stand on each side of her scrutinizing her mercilessly. CLAYTON then extends his hand to her to ask her to dance.)

CLAYTON. Will you join me?
ANNE MARIE. Why, are you coming apart?

(There is a stunned silence. Then CLAYTON howls.)

CLAYTON. Coming apart! Join me! I get it! Someone with a sense of humor! Finally! Let me rephrase that. Will you honor me with this dance?
ANNE MARIE. I'd love to.

(CLAYTON leads her to center stage and motions to the orchestra to begin. All take their positions for: BACH AND BERRY. SIMONE and HENRIETTA have no choice but to dance with each other. They spend the whole dance trying to get close to CLAYTON and ANNE MARIE. During the slow parts of the dance ANN MARIE and CLAYTON are very intent on each other. It is obvious that they are falling in love at first sight. The dance ends. CLAYTON and ANNE MARIE are very close to each other in a sort of trance. The crowd freezes. CLAYTON and ANN MARIE are in spot downstage. The same dialogue, which was inane with the step-sisters, now becomes a transcendant courting ritual. Just as CLAYTON is about to kiss her, she says:)

ANNE MARIE. Well, here we are.
CLAYTON. Nice Ball.
ANNE MARIE. Yes.
CLAYTON. Yes. Nice dance.
ANNE MARIE. Oh, yes. Very nice.

(They start to go in for a kiss.)

CLAYTON. What flowers make you think of a kiss?
ANNE MARIE. I don't know, what?
CLAYTON. Tulips. *(She smiles and begins to go in for the kiss.)* Get it?
ANNE MARIE. I get it. *(They kiss. As they do, the clock begins to strike the hour.)* I hear bells.
CLAYTON. Yes, isn't it wonderful, it's midnight.

ANNE MARIE. *(Dreamily)* Midnight. *(Realizes what is happening and panics at the same moment that the ball comes back to life.)* MIDNIGHT?!!! Oh, my God! I have to run! Thank you, *(Attempts to exit in one direction but is stopped by the crowd. Back to CLAYTON:)* I had a lovely time! Good-bye! I really did! *(Attempts to exit the other way, which is also blocked.)* Oh Goodness Gracious me, I have to get out of here! *(She races from the room up center, and as she does, she loses a slipper.)* Oh, no. Good-bye! Goodbye! I'll always remember this night.

CLAYTON. Wait! Why are you rushing off?

ANNE MARIE. I'm late; I can't explain! Good-bye!

(She's off.)

CLAYTON. Don't go! What's your name? I don't know your name. *(He is in a panic.)* Beauregard! I don't even know her name.

BEAUREGARD. *(As he comes across to CLAYTON he finds the glass slipper and picks it up.)* No one knows her name, Clayton. She was a mystery guest. Look, in her rush, she left this behind. My heavens, it's glass. And look how tiny it is. It must be made especially for her.

CLAYTON. Find her! Find that girl, Beauregard!

BEAUREGARD. But, Clayton, how can we find her? No one knows who she is.

CLAYTON. Find a way, Beauregard! Find her! I have to know who she is! *(He is wild.)* I have to know her better. I think I'm in love with her. *(He begins to circle the ballroom, talking to all the guests.)* Do you know who she is? Did you see her come in? Have you ever seen her before?

(Ad lib, etc.)

BEAUREGARD. But, Clayton, how am I going to find this one girl in all New Orleans?

CLAYTON. That shoe! It's so small, it can only fit her.

BEAUREGARD. But Clayton ...

CLAYTON. I don't care if you have to try that shoe on every female foot in this state! Find her!

ARABELLA. *(Approaching CLAYTON.)* What's the big deal, honey? There's lot of poisson in the sea; if you know what I mean? My little girls, for instance, are both very eligible.

CLAYTON. Out of my way! *(He sweeps her out of the way and continues talking to the crowd.)* I'll offer a reward! My father will pay one thousand dollars to whomever finds this girl.

(Wild excitement from the crowd.)

GOVERNOR BEAUFORT. Now Clayton, I will do not such ...
CLAYTON. Daddy! HELP ME FIND THIS GIRL!!!

(The GOVERNOR is silenced. CLAYTON marches off. The crowd is wild with excitement. The GOVERNOR surveys the Pandemonium for a second, then:)

GOVERNOR BEAUFORT. Beauregard!! FIND THAT GIRL!!! *(The GOVERNOR goes through the crowd.)* We must find this girl! There's a thousand dollar reward!

(Etc. As he starts off.)

BEAUREGARD. *(Following the GOVERNOR.)* Why me? Why do I have to do all the dirty work?

(As they exit, the crowd ad libs and begins to move off.)

Scene Six

(As the curtain comes down on the previous scene, ANNE MARIE and her ANIMALS, transformed back to their previous state, enter in front of it in a crossover. She is wearing one glass slipper. They all stop when ANNE MARIE trips and losses it. They stop to retrieve it.)

ANNE MARIE. Oh, boys! How'd we get ourselves into this mess? The time just flew!
PERIWICKET. We have to hurry, Anne Marie! We have to get home before Arabella and her litter.
ANNE MARIE. You're right, Peri. Lead the way!
PERIWICKET. What do you mean, lead the way?
NICOLAS. You drove here, now get us back!
PERIWICKET. I have no idea where we are. How can I lead us back?
LaFAYETTE. You were the driver! How can you drive here and not know how to get us back? That's silly, even for you, Peri!
PERIWICKET. I don't think I really drove here. That "thing" seemed to drive itself!
NICOLAS. That's ridiculous!
PERIWICKET. Besides, I was trying to get used to being human!

LaFAYETTE. Boy! And you have the nerve to complain that I got us lost!

ANNE MARIE. Now, boys, don't fight. We've got to get home before they do!

PERIWICKET. All right, I'll get us home. *(Stands center stage.)* Eenie, meenie, minie, moe.

LaFAYETTE. Forget it! My "horse" sense tells me we came this way. *(Points right.)* Follow me.

(Exits left.)

ANNE MARIE. Let's hurry, boys. It's only four miles, we can beat them home.

NICOLAS. Cut the chatter! Let's go!

LaFAYETTE. Come on!

ANNE MARIE. Lead the way!

(The all exit.)

Scene Seven

(Back in the kitchen. The scene opens with ANNE MARIE making breakfast, talking with AUNT LULA BELLE, surrounded by LaFAYETTE, PERIWICKET and NICOLAS.)

ANNE MARIE. You should have seen the faces on my "sisters" when I walked in that room.

AUNT LULA BELLE. Oh, I know honey, they must have been green with envy. And they didn't recognize you?

LaFAYETTE. No, they didn't recognize her at all.

NICOLAS. How would you know? We stayed outside with the rest of the horses.

LaFAYETTE. Word gets around in the animal kingdom. I didn't even realize I spoke "horse".

AUNT LULA BELLE. *(To ANNE MARIE.)* Weren't you afraid?

ANNE MARIE. At first, I was petrified.

NICOLAS. It didn't show at all. You carried yourself like a princess.

PERIWICKET. I was afraid; I can tell you. Every time that Simone came near me I got the shivers. And I wasn't even me. I have to say, being human, even for a few hours, was VERY strange. How do you'all do it?

LaFAYETTE. Oh, come on, Peri, it wasn't that bad.

PERIWICKET. For you maybe, you still had four legs. I had to be a man. I didn't know what to do with my hands! And I missed my tail. I was very scared. You, on the other hand, were very brave, Anne Marie.

ANNE MARIE. It was Clayton, he made all the difference. After he asked me to dance, I knew that I would be all right. He's funny, AND he's dreamy. I sure would like to see him again.

(We hear the voices of HENRIETTA and SIMONE offstage as they approach the kitchen. The ANIMALS scamper and hide; but we can see them and they overhear the rest of the scene.)

SIMONE. I really do think that Clayton was very taken with me. He asked me more questions than you.

HENRIETTA. Well, at least I understood his jokes. I thought they were funny.

SIMONE. You did not!

HENRIETTA. I bet you he will ask me out.

SIMONE. Are you crazy! I think he will ask ME out!

(They are about to fight. ANNE MARIE comes between them and begins to serve them breakfast.)

ANNE MARIE. Good morning, girls. It sounds like you enjoyed the ball.

HENRIETTA. Oh, I surely did. But then Clayton asked me to dance.

SIMONE. He did not. You liar. He asked ME to dance.

ANNE MARIE. All right. So you both danced with him. *(A look between them to signify a truce.)* Were there many people there?

SIMONE. Oh yes! Everyone was there.

HENRIETTA. Everyone who is anyone. It's just as well you couldn't come, you would not have fit in at all.

AUNT LULA BELLE. We've heard a rumor that there was a mystery girl there.

SIMONE. Oh yes, I heard something about that.

HENRIETTA. She was nothing in particular. Clayton hardly noticed her.

AUNT LULA BELLE. Oh? We heard that Clayton was enchanted by this mystery girl and that he was heart broken when she ran off at midnight.

SIMONE. That's not true. As a matter of fact, Clayton was dancing with ME when she left. I mean when we heard that she left.

HENRIETTA. You lie! You know very well that he was not dancing at all when she left, not that I noticed, and then he asked ME to dance.

SIMONE. You're the liar. Besides, he said you were too ugly for him to dance with. He told me so while WE were dancing.

HENRIETTA. Ha! You're making it up! He asked ME who the parrot was in the ugly dress, and he pointed right at you!

SIMONE. He did not!

HENRIETTA. Did so!

(Sticks her tongue out at her.)

SIMONE. Did not! I tell you.

(Yanks on her tresses. A real brawl begins. ARABELLA flies into the room. She and ANNE MARIE break up the fight.)

ARABELLA. Girls! Girls! Stop that! There's no time for that now. Beauregard is here. He is trying that stupid glass slipper on every single female foot in greater New Orleans. He is getting out of the carriage. He'll be here any second. *(As she passes ANNE MARIE.)* You, get lost, there's work to be done here. *(ANNE MARIE stands aside but does not leave the room.)* Now girls, primp up a little, please, you both look a fright!

BEAUREGARD. *(O.S.)* All right! Where are they? I don't have all day.

ARABELLA. Here he is. Now think small!

(Enter BEAUREGARD followed by his Lackey.)

BEAUREGARD. I didn't think there were this many feet in the whole state of Louisiana.

ARABELLA. Oh, Mr. Beauregard! How nice it is to see you again. My girls and I had a lovely time at ...

BEAUREGARD. Oh, it's you again.

ARABELLA. Yes, and I really am delighted to ...

BEAUREGARD. Save your breath, honey, it's been a tough day. I have just about seen every foot in New Orleans, and I can tell you, it's not a pretty picture. I'm tired, and I have Clayton waiting in the carriage ...

HENRIETTA & SIMONE. Clayton!

BEAUREGARD. Quiet! And he gets crankier by the minute. We have been everywhere, and no one has even come CLOSE to fitting this shoe. If we don't find this girl soon, Clayton is going to give me a very rough night.

ARABELLA. Well, Mr. Beauregard, your troubles are over. I'm sure one of my two lovely girls will fit the shoe, and marry Clayton, and we'll all live happily ever after.

(Batting eye lashes.)

BEAUREGARD. Ugh! Now there's a thought. All right, you there, *(Pointing at SIMONE.)* Let's see them dogs.

(SIMONE sits. The Lackey positions a small stool in front of her and she hikes up her skirt revealing a very large foot.)

BEAUREGARD. Mercy! *(The Lackey gives BEAUREGARD a helpless look.)* Well, go ahead, Clayton said every foot. *(SIMONE, at first very daintily, attempts to put her huge foot in the slipper. It, of course, does not fit. She tries again, and then a third time. She becomes more and more desperate with each attempt.)* Careful, you, if you break that slipper Clayton will surely kill me.

(SIMONE goes for the shoe one more time. HENRIETTA, who has been anxiously waiting her turn, grabs at the shoe.)

HENRIETTA. Let go of that thing. It's my turn!
SIMONE. Mamma! It's still my turn!
HENRIETTA. Give it up! Your foot's too big!

(She grabs the shoe. A tug of war ensues.)

SIMONE. I can make my foot fit in there. I swear I can!
BEAUREGARD. Hey! Watch that now! That thing is crystal! You're going to smash it.
HENRIETTA. It's my turn!
SIMONE. It is not!
BEAUREGARD. Give me that thing! *(He grabs the slipper.)* Now, if you don't settle down, it won't be anybody's turn, I mean it! *(To SIMONE.)* Your turn is over.

(SIMONE wails and goes to ARABELLA for comfort.)

ARABELLA. *(Initially very cold to her.)* I told you to think small. *(SIMONE wails even louder.)* There, there. Someday, your prince will come, I suppose.

(As ARABELLA begins to comfort her; BEAUREGARD throws her shoe at her, hitting her skirt, which silences her immediately. BEAUREGARD gives the glass slipper back to The Lackey.)

HENRIETTA. *(She positions herself on the same chair where SIMONE had tried on the slipper.)* All right! My turn!

(The Lackey looks at her then at BEAUREGARD. He is plainly scared of HENRIETTA.)

BEAUREGARD. Oh boy! I better do this myself. *(He takes the slipper from the Lackey as he approaches HENRIETTA.)* You touch this shoe and this fitting is over, you hear me?

(HENRIETTA begins to go through the same motions as SIMONE.)

ARABELLA. *(After the second try.)* Henrietta, cheri, you are not thinking small enough. I mean TRES PETITE, honey child. Now try again!
HENRIETTA. I am trying Mamma; but there is really something wrong with this shoe. It fit me so well last night.
ARABELLA. Here let me help you.

(She steps over BEAUREGARD.)

BEAUREGARD. Oh no you don't ...
ARABELLA. Out of my way Beauregard, I mean business.

(She sweeps BEAUREGARD out of the way. Grabs the slipper and positions herself to help.)

HENRIETTA. Push Mammy, Push!
ARABELLA. Now here we go! *(They try again and it still will not fit.)* I don't know what's wrong with you two. In my day, if a girl needed to think small, she just DID it. Now move over, let me try.

(She pushes HENRIETTA off the stool and sits to try on the slipper.)

BEAUREGARD. Now, wait a minute here!
ARABELLA. Beauregard, I'm trying on this here shoe. If it fits, that Clayton better watch out.
BEAUREGARD. But you are already married!
ARABELLA. Nobody's perfect. All right girls, lend a hand here.

(HENRIETTA and SIMONE attempt to help ARABELLA put on the shoe. There is a bit of a melee as both BEAUREGARD and The Lackey dive in and retrieve the shoe from them.)

BEAUREGARD. Well, I never! You, madam, are a disgrace! And don't think I won't tell the Governor about this little episode.
ARABELLA. Can it, you twerp!

(She picks up the cushion on which the glass slipper was resting and hits BEAUREGARD over the head with it.)

BEAUREGARD. Well! *(BEAUREGARD draws himself up and begins a long cross to exit. As he is about to reach the door AUNT LULA BELLE stands in his way.)* What do YOU want?
AUNT LULA BELLE. There is another unmarried female in this house.
BEAUREGARD. Oh, Brother! Not you too!
AUNT LULA BELLE. No. Not me, you imbecile. My niece Anne Marie.
BEAUREGARD. *(Taking a look at her.)* Oh no. I remember you. I really don't have this kind of time. I tell you Clayton is VERY cranky.
AUNT LULA BELLE. You are supposed to be trying that shoe on every unmarried foot in this parish, and you are not going anywhere until Anne Marie gets her turn.
ARABELLA. Let the man go, you silly old woman!

(She begins to approach AUNT LULA BELLE. AUNT LULA BELLE grabs a broom and barricades the door.)

AUNT LULA BELLE. *(Speaking with hereto unknown strength.)* I said nobody moves. And I ain't just whistling Dixie. Now, Anne Marie, try on that shoe!
BEAUREGARD. Oh, all right. If Clayton is going to kill me, I might as well give him a reason. Come over here girlie. Let's get this over with.

(ANNE MARIE sits on the stool and presents her foot. BEAUREGARD hesitates for a moment as he notices how small the foot is. Just as he is about to try on the shoe, CLAYTON thunders in.)

CLAYTON. Beauregard! What is going on! How long do you plan to keep me waiting! Well?!

(He sees ANNE MARIE; and that BEAUREGARD is about to try the

shoe on her. For some reason, which he does not understand, he is transfixed by her. He does not recognize her, but there is something magnetic about her.)

BEAUREGARD. Sorry, Clayton, we have had a delay. This will only take a second and then we'll go.

(BEAUREGARD notices CLAYTON's odd reaction to ANNE MARIE.)

CLAYTON. Go ahead.

(BEAUREGARD slowly approaches the foot with the slipper and slips it on without any effort.)

BEAUREGARD. Oh, my heavens, it fits. The shoe fits! *(Gets up and declaims:)* THE SHOE FITS!

(There's general ad lib of surprise. ARABELLA and the girls are dumbstruck. AUNT LULA BELLE is very proud. The ANIMALS come out of their hiding places with loud ad libs. BEAUREGARD is petrified.)

CLAYTON. You? Is it really you?
ANNE MARIE. Yes. It's me. *(Taking the other slipper out of her apron pocket.)* And here's the companion.
CLAYTON. But how?
ANNE MARIE. Clayton, do you believe in magic?
CLAYTON. I do if you are the girl.
ANNE MARIE. I am the girl.
CLAYTON. *(Not quite convinced.)* Will you join me?
ANNE MARIE. Why, are you coming apart?
CLAYTON. What flowers make you think of a kiss?
ANNE MARIE. Tulips.
CLAYTON. My Heavens, it IS you. *(He rushes to her and takes her in his arms. He is about to kiss her. Stops.)* What's your name?
ANNE MARIE. Anne Marie Louise De Ville.
CLAYTON. Anne Marie Louise De Ville. That's a beautiful name. *(He kisses her.)* Will you marry me?
ANNE MARIE. Yes.

(A wild reaction from everybody. They all hug her and kiss her, then:)

ARABELLA. I always knew it. I'm so happy for you. *(Goes to her.)* My own daughter!

AUNT LULA BELLE. Now, wait a minute!

HENRIETTA. My sister! I knew it all along!

SIMONE. We were teasing you before. We tend to kid a little hard, Mamma always said ... Can you ever forgive us?

AUNT LULA BELLE. You have no shame! *(To ANNE MARIE.)* You don't owe them anything.

ANNE MARIE. *(Thinks about it for a second. Then to the girls.)* Of course I forgive you.

(Squeals of delight from both sisters.)

SIMONE. Oh, thank you, Anne Marie!

HENRIETTA. We always secretly liked you.

SIMONE. And I would be happy to be the Maid of Honor.

AUNT LULA BELLE. Now, just one cotton picking minute ...

HENRIETTA. *(Charging through LULA BELLE.)* No, I'm the oldest sister, I get to be the Maid of Honor!

SIMONE. What has that got to do with it? She likes me best!

HENRIETTA. She does not!

SIMONE. She does too! She thinks you're ugly and she'll never forgive you for breaking her dolls.

HENRIETTA. At least I didn't nail her pet lizard to the wall.

SIMONE. That was an accident! Really Anne Marie

AUNT LULA BELLE. Accident my foot! Show them you tail Peri.

PERIWICKET. Aunt Lula Belle, Please!

ANNE MARIE. Girls, Everybody! We need to try to get along, all of us. Now, I would like both of you to be Maids of Honor. *(Girls squeal. AUNT LULA BELLE sulks.)* You too Aunt Lula Belle.

(LULA BELLE beams and kisses ANNE MARIE.)

CLAYTON. Let's go back to the Hotel Pontchartrain and tell my Daddy. I want to get married as soon as possible.

ANNE MARIE. I can't wait to meet your Daddy.

CLAYTON. Lead the way Beauregard.

(Before BEAUREGARD has a chance to react, ARABELLA grabs him and takes him out.)

ARABELLA. Come on Beauregard! *(As she leads him out.)* Have you ever been married?

(They exit amidst ad libs. Everyone laughs and follows, the

ANIMALS taking AUNT LULA BELLE out as they ad lib congratulations to her. SIMONE and HENRIETTA are the last out and attempt to exit at the same time, and bump each other.)

HENRIETTA. Oh, my dear, please, you go first.
SIMONE. No, no. I insist, you go first.
HENRIETTA. Absolutely not. After you.
SIMONE. Age before beauty.
HENRIETTA. Pearls before swine.

(She starts to exit.)
SIMONE. Why you little ...

(Is about to attack her.)

BEAUREGARD. *(Reentering exasperated.)* Ladies! *(The girls draw themselves up, give BEAUREGARD a withering look and exit arm in arm at the same time.)* Oh, brother!

Scene Eight

(The scene shifts back to The Hotel Pontchartrain Ballroom, which is now decorated for the wedding. The crowd is waiting in anticipation. Music plays.)

GOVERNOR BEAUFORT. *(Entering unexpectedly. The crowd murmurs.)* Ladies and Gentlemen, your attention please! I know you expect to see the beautiful bride and not me, but there is an announcement that I have to make. As you know, it is now common knowledge that my beautiful daughter-in-law to be, Anne Marie Louise de Ville, was the mystery warrior who helped win the battle for our fair city. Well, war heroes seem to run in the family. We have just learned that her father, General Gaston de Ville, has returned from Mississippi, and while he was there, he secured three counties against the advancing Yankees. *(Cheering from the crowd.)* General de Ville has returned just in time to give his beautiful daughter away! Now Clayton. *(CLAYTON enters and stands waiting for his bride.)* Beauregard!

(BEAUREGARD, who will officiate, enters and assumes his place. The GOVERNOR sits. The processional begins. NICOLAS and LaFAYETTE in formal clothes, enter scattering flower petals, followed by PERIWICKET, also in formal clothes, who escorts

ARABELLA to her seat. Then SIMONE makes her way down the aisle followed by HENRIETTA and finally by AUNT LULA BELLE, all three beautifully dressed as bridesmaids. Then there is a fanfare and everyone stands and turns to watch as ANNE MARIE, on the arm of her father, enters to Mendelsohn's wedding march. As she reaches CLAYTON, her father hands her to him and sits with the GOVERNOR.)

[FOREVERMORE]

CLAYTON.
FOREVERMORE, I TAKE YOU ANNE TO BE MY LOVING WIFE

ANNE MARIE & CLAYTON.
I PROMISE THAT I'LL LOVE YOU ALL MY LIFE

FOREVERMORE, THIS IS HOW I WANTED IT TO BE

ANNE MARIE.
ALL OF US TOGETHER LIKE A FAMILY SHOULD BE

ALL.
FOREVERMORE, STORMS WE'LL WEATHER
FOREVERMORE, ALL TOGETHER
FOREVERMORE, WE'VE FOUND LOVE

ANNE MARIE & CLAYTON.
I FOUND THE ONE THAT I'VE BEEN DREAMING OF

(Just as they are about to kiss, as the song is ending, and BEAUREGARD is about to begin the ceremony; there is a huge explosion and puff of smoke, and The FAIRY GODMOTHER appears out of thin air. Music begins.)

FAIRY GODMOTHER. Oh, boy. It is really getting thick in here. I thought I was watching an episode of little maison dans le prairie. *(Looking at CLAYTON.)* Hey, sweetie, he's a hunk!
ANNE MARIE. Oh, Fairy Godmother, you came back!
FAIRY GODMOTHER. Of course I came back. I heard you were getting hitched so I flew in to preside over the ceremony.
ANNE MARIE. Can you do that?
FAIRY GODMOTHER. Of course I can, I'm a Justice of the

Peace in the off season.
    BEAUREGARD. *(Moving out of the way.)* Best of luck, honey.
    FAIRY GODMOTHER. Now you stand over here.
    ANNE MARIE. Here?
    FAIRY GODMOTHER. And you over here handsome.

[A LITTLE O' DIS, A LITTLE O' DAT] (Reprise)

FAIRY GODMOTHER.
A LITTLE O' DIS, A LITTLE O' DAT
WE GONNA MAKE YOU HUSBAND AND WIFE IN NO TIME
    FLAT
YOU HOLDING DE HANDS
YOU SPEAKING DE VOWS
AND IT'S HAPPY EVER AFTER TIME RIGHT NOW

Now, let's see

YOU TAKE THIS HANDSOME MAN HERE
TO BE YOUR LOVER MAN?

    ANNE MARIE. I do!

    FAIRY GODMOTHER.
DO YOU PROMISE TO LOVE THIS GIRL FOR THE REST OF
    YOUR LIFE?

    CLAYTON. I do!

    FAIRY GODMOTHER.
NOW TAKE HER IN YOUR ARMS NOW
AND GIVE HER A BIG SMOOCH
DAT'S DE WAY. OK! NOW
I PRONOUNCE YOU MAN AND WIFE

END

www.ingramcontent.com/pod-product-compliance
Lightning Source LLC
Chambersburg PA
CBHW070402120726
47909CB00008B/2956